WHEN I GROW UP

For the real Zachary and his sister, Amy – L.G.

For Neddy, with love – J.J.

First published in 2000 by Macmillan Children's Books
A division of Macmillan Publishers Limited
25 Eccleston Place, London SW1W 9NF
Basingstoke and Oxford
Associated companies throughout the world
www.panmacmillan.com

ISBN 0 333 90177 0 HB
ISBN 0 333 90190 8 PB

Text copyright © 2000 Lennie Goodings
Illustrations copyright © 2000 Jenny Jones
Moral rights asserted

1 3 5 7 9 8 6 4 2

A CIP catalogue record for this book is available from the British Library.

Printed in Belgium by Proost.

When I Grow Up

Written by Lennie Goodings

Illustrated by Jenny Jones

MACMILLAN
CHILDREN'S BOOKS

Zachary and his mum
have the same colour fur
and the same colour eyes.

They both like a hug and they both like
chocolate ice cream with honey on top.
In the morning they are both yawning,
sleepy-eyed sleepyheads.
Zachary says, when he grows up,
he's going to live with his mum.
Mum says that's all right with her.
But . . .

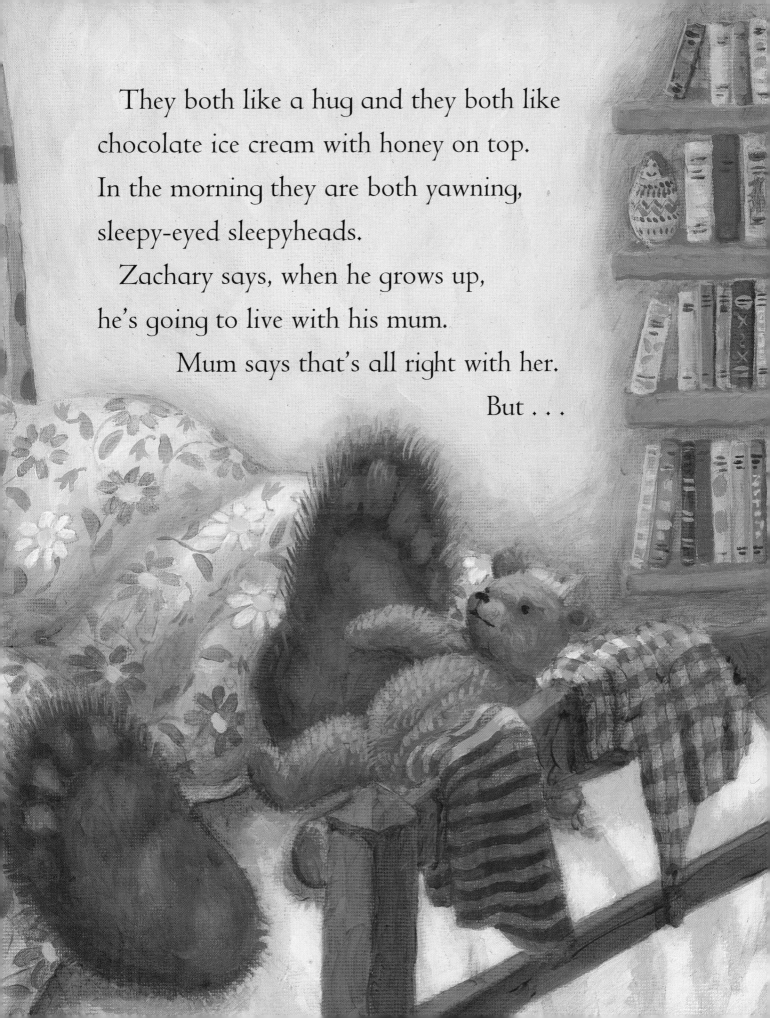

"Maybe," says Mum, "when you grow up, you'll be a famous footballer."

"Oh, yes!" says Zachary. "I could score all the goals and be a hero! And then I'll come back and live with you."

"Or maybe," says Mum,
"when you grow up,
you might be a baker."

"Mmm!" says Zachary. "And I'll make sticky chocolate birthday cakes every single day."

"Will you let me lick the bowl?" asks Mum.

"I might," laughs Zachary. "And then I'll come back and live with you."

"Maybe," says Mum, "when you grow up,
you'll be a pilot and fly a helicopter."
"That would be great," says Zachary.
"I'd go high up over the clouds."
"Oh, yes!" says Mum.
"And then I'll come back and live
with you."

"Or maybe," says Mum, "you'll be an ambulance driver and save someone's life."

"Yes!" says Zachary, "and I'll zoom through the streets with the siren going and the lights flashing. And then I'll come back and live with you."

"Or maybe," says Mum, "you'll be a cowboy and ride a big horse."

"Yippee," says Zachary. "And I'd lasso cows with a rope.

"And then I'd be made sheriff and I'd have a shiny star and a big hat."

"Oooh!" says Mum.

"And I'd catch all the baddies and throw them in jail," says Zachary. "And then I'll come back and live with you."

"Or maybe," says Mum, "you'll be a farmer with a red tractor and you'd drive round and round the fields."

"I think it should be blue," says Zachary.

"Oh?" says Mum.

"Yes, blue, because that's my favourite colour!

"And I'd have a big friendly dog and he'd help me look after my sheep," says Zachary. "And then I'll come back and live with you."

"Or maybe," says Mum, "you'll be a magician and make rabbits jump out of hats."

"Oh, yes!" says Zachary. "I could make you disappear!"

"Oh, no!" says Mum.

"But I'll make you appear again. And then I'll come back and live with you."

"Maybe," says Mum, "you'll be a daddy
and have a little cub just like you."

"I might . . ." says Zachary. "And then . . .

. . . we'll all live next door to you!"

Also illustrated by Jenny Jones:

Danny and the Great White Bear

MACMILLAN CHILDREN'S BOOKS